A MOON,
A STAR,
A STORY

An Anthology
of New Stories

Other Story Collections from Blackie

Let's Share a Story

Storyworld

The Magic Kiss

A MOON, A STAR, A STORY

An Anthology of New Stories

Illustrated by Toni Goffe

Blackie

British Library Cataloguing in Publication Data
A Moon, a star, a story.
  I. Goffe, Toni
  823′.914 [J]

ISBN 0-216-92759-5

Blackie and Son Ltd
7 Leicester Place
London WC2H 7BP

Printed in Hong Kong

Contents

Special Offer

Caroline Pitcher

'I'll do the shopping, Mum,' said Sarah. 'You have a rest on that chair by the Exit!'

'What a wonderful idea. I am very tired. Here's the shopping list,' said Sarah's mum.

'BRRRM BRRRM!' roared Sarah as she raced around the supermarket with the trolley.

Sarah looked at the list. It said PIE.

She reached down into the freezer and grabbed what looked like a chicken pie. She dropped it into the trolley.

Sarah looked at the list again. It was fluttering. A lot of blackbirds had settled all round the edge of the shopping trolley, flapping their wings.

'Four-and-twenty blackbirds, dear, all present and correct,' squawked the bird nearest to Sarah.

'Why?' asked Sarah.

'Why? Pie, that's why,' he squawked. 'We were baked in it. Look, now it's open.'

Sure enough the box was open and there was flakey pastry all over the trolley.

'Can you sing?' asked Sarah.

'Of course we can!' cried the blackbird.

Twenty-four blackbirds threw their heads back and burst into 'Sing a Song of Sixpence'.

Sarah looked at her list again. It said MILK.

'I should buy the bottle with the gold top if I were you,' said a low voice like a foghorn right in her ear. 'It's the creamiest. It's the best. I should know. It's mine.'

Sarah turned round. There stood a pretty Jersey cow with eyes as dark as treacle toffee and a buttercup sticking out of her mouth.

'Good afternoon. I am the Cow who jumps over the Moon,' she explained.

'Where is it, then?' asked Sarah, gazing up.

'Don't be silly, dear, you can't see it properly in the daytime,' lowed the cow. She stood up on her back legs and placed her neat little front hooves in the trolley. With much puffing and lowing and blowing she heaved herself in. Then she called, 'Come on, then,' to a small ginger shape on the top of the fridge.

The small ginger shape leaped down and landed between her curly horns.

It was a ginger cat. It was holding a small violin in one paw and a bow in another. It watched the blackbirds and licked its lips.

'Oh no! It's the cat and the fiddle!' squawked the blackbirds. 'Please don't bring that little dog. He never stops laughing. Gets on your nerves.'

'The little dog is on the pet food shelf today,' explained the cow. 'And the dish and the spoon are next to cutlery.'

'Good,' sang the blackbirds. 'You had a narrow escape there, Sarah. You're very lucky.'

Sarah looked at the list. It said JAM TARTS.

She found them on the cake shelf and had just put the packet on the cow's velvety back when a voice whispered, 'Raspberry jam . . . an excellent choice!'

Sarah turned round. There stood a young man with straight hair down to his shoulders. He wore a hat like an upside-down flowerpot and a tunic covered with red hearts. He had tights which were far too big for him. They were all wrinkled round his ankles.

'You must be the Knave of Hearts,' said Sarah.

'At your service,' he smiled, and bowed low.

'It's all lies, of course,' he whispered. 'I never stole those tarts.'

'You did!' screeched the blackbirds. 'Did DID DID!'

'Excuse me,' said Sarah. 'What are you all doing in this supermarket?'

The cow took a deep breath and explained. 'You see, children watch television and videos now and don't know their Nursery Rhymes. We Nursery Rhyme Characters are becoming an Endangered Species. We must get out and about and into people's homes. So we are on Free Offer. For example, with a packet of fish fingers, you get the fish who bites this little finger on your right.'

'Sounds rather painful,' said Sarah, frowning.

She looked at the list. It said EGGS.

'Ah! I thought it might be you,' she smiled, as Humpty Dumpty climbed very carefully down from the egg shelf.

He was fat and quite bald. He had on a pair of trousers with a red and yellow zig-zag pattern that made your eyes go funny. They were held up by purple braces. He had a bow tie with red spots. It kept spinning round. On his head was a peaked cap with EGGSTRA SPECIAL written on it.

'Pray make room for me in the trolley, Knave of Hearts,' said Humpty Dumpty in a trembling voice.

'Why should I make room for a fat egg with no sense of balance?' jeered the Knave. 'I hope you *do* fall. I fancy some scrambled eggs.'

'Oh, come on,' said Sarah. 'This trolley is so heavy. You and the cow should walk.'

'Of course, Sarah,' lowed the cow politely. She jumped down from the trolley with the cat and fiddle still perched between her horns.

The Knave climbed down with a very bad grace. He sulked, and would not walk properly. Instead, he rested one foot on the bar at the bottom of the trolley and sort of scooted along.

Humpty Dumpty sat in the part meant for toddlers.

Sarah looked at her list. It said CURD CHEESE.

Hurray! Mum was going to make a cheesecake.

She licked her lips as she helped herself to a large tub of curd cheese and put it next to Humpty Dumpty.

'AAAAGH!' he screamed, pointing at the tub. 'A monster. AAAAGH!'

There, crouched on the lid, was an enormous black spider. He grinned at poor Humpty and began to tap-dance, waving his eight legs with their hairy little knee-caps at Humpty's horrified face.

Before Sarah could do anything, a pretty girl with curly blonde hair and a flower-sprigged dress jumped into the trolley and put her arm round the sobbing egg.

'I'll look after you, poor egg,' she said. 'My name is Miss Muffet. I can never get my curds and whey eaten because of that wretched spider, but I can tell that *you're* even more frightened than I am.'

'You can look after *me* if you like, dear,' whispered the Knave of Hearts craftily. 'I'll sit on a tuffet with you any time you like.'

'No thank you,' said Miss Muffet primly. 'I've heard all about you, Knave.'

'Behave yourselves,' said Sarah.

Sarah set off towards the Fresh Fruit counter but stopped suddenly. There was a strange sound of thundering hooves.

Over the display of fruit there hung a large cardboard banana. Everyone knew it was a banana, except the cow. She thought it was the crescent moon and galloped at it from every direction, trying to jump over it. But the cow was too plump and the banana too high.

Every time she jumped she knocked down more fruit with her little hooves. Apples, peaches, plums and pineapples went spilling and rolling all over the floor.

'Stop all that noise!' cried Sarah to the blackbirds who had their wings over their ears but were screeching at the cat and the fiddle, 'Boo! Don't call us, we'll call you!'

The cat became so angry that he stopped sawing away at his fiddle, swung it round his head and threw it at them, but they all flew up in the air and he hit Humpty Dumpty instead.

'This is the end,' screamed Humpty, clutching at the big hole in his shell. 'It's no use calling all the King's horses and all the King's men – '

'Because THEY CAN'T PUT HIM TOGETHER AGAIN!' shouted everyone.

'No, but extra-strong glue can,' cried Sarah, dashing for a tube from the stationery shelf. Humpty Dumpty lay waving his little red and yellow legs in the air while she glued back the piece of shell.

But worse was yet to come. Sarah heard someone roaring, 'Stop him! Stop thief!' Spinning round she saw the Knave of Hearts being chased by the Supermarket Supervisor – a great big woman with a furious face and steam coming out of her ears. The great big woman grabbed hold of the Knave,

14

turned him upside down and shook. Out of his tunic fell packets and packets of jam tarts, raspberry tarts, strawberry, blackcurrant, even lemon curd.

As if this wasn't enough, he had a large packet of frozen puff pastry and a jar of cherry jam to make more tarts at home.

Sarah could see her mother's horrified face staring at them from the other side of the check-out. The adventure had turned into a nightmare.

'I don't want those Nursery Rhymes, even if they are free!' she cried to the woman at the till.

'But you've got to have us, got to, GOT TO!' screamed the blackbirds, the cow, the cat, the Knave, Miss Muffet and the spider. Humpty Dumpty just sobbed so that a great big puddle of tears spread across the floor.

'Don't know what all the fuss is about,' said the woman at the till. 'The offer closed yesterday.'

'But what can we do? Where can we go?' wailed the Nursery Rhymes. 'We'll just fade away. No one will ever hear of us again.'

Sarah felt very sorry for them all, even though they were such a nuisance.

Humpty's tears had splashed all over her shoes. 'We're homeless,' he sobbed. 'Nobody wants us.'

'Yes they do,' said a little voice. 'I want you. I'll give you a home. But you'll have to behave yourselves. No nonsense, no noise, no fighting and NO STEALING.'

'Of course, yer honour,' simpered the Knave bowing low to a little man in the queue. It was Mr Ticket the Librarian.

'You will live in the Children's Library in a display and perform every day at twelve o'clock. There will be big pink cushions for the children to sit on and listen.'

'Hurray!' they all shouted, and lined up, meek and mild.

And out they all went. The Knave was carrying Mr Ticket's groceries.

'There's another free offer tomorrow if you're interested,' called the Supervisor as Sarah and her Mother were leaving. 'It's Fairy Tales.'

'Oh, no!' cried Sarah. 'That means the Three Bears with a packet of porridge oats and a Giant with every tin of Baked Beans. We'll be shopping somewhere else!'

The Circus Prince

Saviour Pirotta

Prince Oregano lived in a castle with his mother and father. The castle was beautiful. It had flags and turrets and a real drawbridge that could go up and down. Oregano was very pleased with it.

On Oregano's birthday a princess called Salmonella came to see him. Princess Salmonella was jealous of Prince Oregano's drawbridge. She thought it was the best drawbridge in the world. But she didn't say so. Instead she sniffed haughtily and looked around the big rooms. 'Your castle is nothing compared to mine,' she boasted. 'Mine has a cupboard full of ghosts.'

Prince Oregano had never heard of ghosts that lived in cupboards before. He thought maybe he had some, too. The palace was full of old furniture. Princess Salmonella helped him look all over the castle. But they found nothing in the wardrobes except piles of old shoes.

'Oh, dear,' said Princess Salmonella, pretending to be disappointed. 'I don't think much of your castle at all.'

Then a horrible duchess called Malicia came to see Oregano. She, too, was jealous of Oregano's beautiful castle. Her father, you see, did not let her fly flags on her own.

'Your castle is a diddly old thing,' sniffed Duchess Malicia. 'Mine has a dungeon full of roaring lions.'

Prince Oregano was very upset. 'My castle is better than yours,' he shouted. And he badgered his mother into taking him down to the dungeons just to see if there were any roaring lions living there. Of course, he found nothing except a pile of mouldy old storybooks someone had thrown away.

Poor Prince Oregano's birthday was spoilt. All through the day he could think of nothing except Princess Salmonella's haunted cupboard and Lady Malicia's dungeon full of roaring lions. He didn't even say thank you to his parents for their lovely presents.

'I want a cupboard full of ghosts and a dungeon full of lions,' he said. And he dropped his presents on the floor where the servants would trip over them.

In the afternoon some people from the local circus came to entertain the royal family. There were acrobats and fire-eaters. Seals rode around the room on funny little bicycles. The clowns made everyone laugh, too. Only Prince Oregano sat on his throne and sulked.

When the show was over, the King invited the circus people to tea in the main hall. They accepted immediately. The clowns gobbled up all the jellies and the cakes. They drank all the lemonade at once. Only the seals sat politely in their chairs until the servants offered them some biscuits.

'Dear me,' said the Queen, who normally took a whole evening to finish a cup of tea. 'Our subjects do seem to be hungry, don't they?'

Oregano said nothing. He was still upset. The Queen sighed wearily and turned to speak to a clown who was spilling jam all over her new sofa. Oregano wandered away alone. 'Maybe I should run away,' he thought to himself. 'Then they'll all be sorry for not giving me what I want.'

Oregano looked out of the window. It was raining outside. 'Maybe I should hide somewhere in the palace,' the Prince thought. 'That will teach them all right.'

Oregano crept into the kitchen. There was no one around except the cook's cat and a budgie in a cage. Oregano went to the kitchen table and peeped under the tablecloth. It was dark under there. A perfect hiding-place. Oregano crawled in.

'Hello,' said a boy's voice in the dark. 'You seem to be rather upset.'

Oregano looked around him in alarm. 'Get out,' he said to the voice. 'This is my table.'

The voice laughed. And a small bell tinkled with it.

'You're a clown,' Oregano gasped.

'So I am,' said the clown. 'Only I wish I was a prince. Then I could live in your beautiful castle and raise the drawbridge every day.'

'It's not much fun, really,' grumbled Prince Oregano. 'I'd rather live somewhere else.'

'I bet you wouldn't want to be a clown, though,' said the voice. 'Then you'd have to sleep in a small caravan with ghosts in the cupboard and lions roaring in your ears.'

'That's exactly what I want,' cried Prince Oregano.

'Then maybe we should change places,' said the clown.

'I could be a prince and you can be a clown.'

'I'd like that very much,' said Prince Oregano without thinking.

The clown lifted the tablecloth for a second. Oregano saw him pull a twig out of his pocket. Then he dropped the tablecloth again.

'Repeat the spell after me,' said the clown. He waved the twig about and sang:

> Magic magic in the air
> change the Prince into a clown
> let the clown become a prince
> make him wear a golden crown

Prince Oregano repeated the spell. Suddenly he felt drowsy. He yawned. The clown put the twig away. 'Goodbye, little Prince,' he whispered.

No one can tell how long Prince Oregano slept. But when he woke up it was late at night. The moon was shining through the window. 'That's funny,' Prince Oregano thought. 'I've never seen the moon through my window before.'

Just then he moved his head and a bell tinkled. Oregano felt the collar round his neck. Suddenly, he remembered. Of course, he wasn't in the palace any more now. He was living in the clown's caravan, with the haunted cupboard and the lions roaring in his ears.

Oregano jumped out of bed and ran to the cupboard. He pulled it open. Yaaaaaah. Oregano nearly jumped out of his skin. The cupboard was full of ghosts.

'Help,' Prince Oregano shouted.

The ghosts swooped out. They danced around the room. One of them dropped some bones on the floor and started playing pick-ups. Oregano hid under his blanket and watched. When the sun came up the ghosts disappeared into the wardrobe. The door slammed shut after them.

Prince Oregano heard a loud roar. He remembered the lions. Quickly, he put on his slippers and ran out. The lions were sitting in a cage. Oregano fed them some apples. He filled their dish with water. The lions showed him their teeth and flicked their tails. Prince Oregano squealed with excitement.

Soon it was time for breakfast. An old woman came to the caravan and gave Prince Oregano a piece of mouldy bread. 'I don't like mouldy bread,' Prince Oregano cried. 'I want some porridge with golden honey on top.'

The old woman threw the bread on the floor. 'This is the only thing there is,' she said. 'Golden honey indeed. What do you think you are. A prince?'

'But I *am* a prince,' said Oregano.

The woman snorted. 'Get your clothes on, clown,' she said. 'We got a show to do this morning.' And she slammed the door shut before Prince Oregano had time to explain.

The poor Prince did not know what to do. He'd never played the clown before. Slowly he put on his clothes and went to the big tent. It was freezing. And his costume was full of holes.

Prince Oregano was pushed out into the ring. A clown hit him on the head with a plastic hammer. Another one drenched him in dirty water.

'Uggh!' Prince Oregano was soaked.

'Get a move on,' cried the ringmaster. 'I'm not paying you to stand around.'

Prince Oregano tried to explain who he was. But it was in vain. No one would listen. The clowns drenched him in water again. They made him jump up and down on a smelly mattress. The audience laughed their heads off.

After the show, Prince Oregano went back to the caravan. He opened the cupboard and the ghosts flew out. But they weren't so scary now that he had seen them before. The lions in their cages roared for their dinner. But Prince Oregano did not go out to watch. It's funny how exciting things can seem ordinary when you've seen them already.

That night the circus left town. Prince Oregano travelled far away to many countries. Soon he became used to the life of a clown. The circus folk showed him how to do cartwheels and somersaults. They taught him how to juggle. The children liked his show.

But deep inside his heart, Oregano missed his beautiful castle. He missed his flags and his drawbridge. And he couldn't think of his mum and dad without bursting into tears.

One day the circus stopped in a field. The circus folk erected the tent. A large crowd gathered at the ticket booth.

'The royal family are coming to see our show,' the performers said excitedly. 'We must do our best.'

When the show started Prince Oregano jumped into the ring. The audience yelled. Prince Oregano made a rubber duck come out of his hat and blew soap bubbles in the air.

The royal family clapped politely. Oregano turned to give them a bow. Then he froze.

'What's the matter?' asked the juggler.

Oregano pointed to the royal family. There, sitting on their portable thrones were his mother and father. And right next to them was the little clown wearing the prince's crown.

Tears came to Oregano's eyes. 'Hello, Mum,' he shouted at the Queen. 'Hello, Dad.'

The King and Queen looked uneasy. The little clown slipped out of his throne.

'Excuse this stupid clown, Your Majesty,' said the ringmaster. And he grabbed Oregano by the ears and threw him out of the ring. The crowds thought it was all part of the show. They cheered and clapped.

Oregano was so ashamed he crawled under the table to hide. If only his mother and father could recognise him. Then he could go back to his castle.

'Hello,' said a voice in the dark. 'Didn't you like your wishes after all?'

It was the little clown speaking.

'Ghosts and lions are fun,' said the prince. 'But my castle and my family are better still.'

'Drawbridges are fine, too,' said the clown. 'But they're not half as much fun as working in the circus.'

He took the twig out of his pocket and started singing again.

> Magic magic in the air
> change the Prince into a clown
> let the clown become a prince
> make him wear a golden crown

Prince Oregano repeated the spell after him. Then he fell asleep.

When he woke up it was night-time. Prince Oregano rubbed his eyes. That was funny, he couldn't see the moon out of the window tonight. He sat up. A woman hurried into the room. It was the maid.

'Your Majesty,' she said. 'Would you like a glass of milk and some biscuits?'

Prince Oregano leapt out of bed and danced around the room. 'I'm back,' he shouted. 'I've come home again.'

The maid laughed. 'You've never gone missing Your Highness.'

'Oh yes, I have,' shouted Prince Oregano. 'That was a clown sleeping in my bed. We exchanged places on my last birthday.'

The maid hurried out of the room. 'What stories princes tell nowadays!' she said to herself.

Oregano realized that no one would believe he'd become a clown, just like no one at the circus had believed he was a prince. He decided to keep the secret to himself.

At dawn he went to the front door of the castle and raised the drawbridge. He never wished for a cupboard full of ghosts or a dungeon packed with roaring lions again. He was quite happy as he was.

Marika's Favourite Story

Jenny Koralek

Marika loved going to spend the night with her grannie. She lived in a flat with a long narrow hall where Marika could play skittles before supper.

Supper was different from supper at home. At home Marika had baked beans on toast, or scrambled egg at the kitchen table. But at Grannie's she sat in the dining-room on a beautiful old chair at a beautiful shiny table. She had a mat of her own with pictures of huntsmen on it and even a little mat under her glass of apple juice. Grannie gave her a plate with ham rolled up and radishes and crisp white rolls speckled with poppyseed. Round the ham she made patterns in strips of sliced red peppers and green peppers. For pudding Marika had a bowl of nuts and raisins and a bunch of grapes or a satsuma from the fruit bowl.

When she got down from supper she always went to the sitting-room, straight to Grannie's glass cabinet – a small cupboard full of windows – to stare at all the treasures. There were fans made of ivory and pieces of lace as fine as a cobweb.

There were cups and saucers painted with gold. There was a china shepherdess and a china cow. There was a little silver chair and a box in the shape of a heart with 'I love you' written on it in spidery writing. And last, not least, there was the little wooden cat.

Marika and Grannie would look at every single thing very carefully, always leaving the little wooden cat till last, and then Marika would sit down on the stool by Grannie in her chair and say, 'Now, please, Grannie, tell me again. Tell me my favourite story.'

'Are you sure you want the same story?' asked Grannie.

'I am sure,' said Marika.

'All right,' said Grannie. 'Long ago there was a little girl called Marika . . .'

'And she was your mother, wasn't she, Grannie?'

'Yes. My mother, who lived in a beautiful city . . .'

'Where all the churches had domes like onions instead of towers,' said Marika, 'but onions made of gold . . .'

'Yes,' said Grannie. 'And Marika lived with her mother and father near the river by the bridge . . .'

'And that Marika's mother was called Marika, too, like you, Grannie, and me. We are a long chain of Marikas . . .'

'Yes,' said Grannie. 'Who's telling this story to who?'

'I was just starting you off,' said Marika.

'One day Marika fell ill. She had a very bad cough

32

and it just would not go away, so her mother and father took her to the mountains to stay with . . .'

'Another Marika!' said Marika happily. 'Your mother's mother's mother!'

'Yes,' said Grannie. 'Old Marika. She lived on a farm far away from the town . . . all by herself except for her cow and her horse and cart, and her chickens and her pig and her apple trees and her grapevine.

'Little Marika soon felt much better up there in the fresh air. Old Marika taught her how to make butter and cheese, and to pick apples and grapes and let her feed the chickens and collect the warm eggs every morning from the nests.

'One day she said, "Tomorrow is market day and you must come to town with me."

'Next morning, old Marika harnessed her horse to her cart and little Marika helped her put all the butter, eggs, cheese and fruit into the cart.

'And off they went to market. The town was very small. There was a square in the middle with a fountain and a church and a few shops.

'Little Marika was very excited. She had not been to town for a long time.

'"Oh," she cried. "Can I go shopping now, Grannie?"

'"No," said old Marika. "First you must help me unload the cart and put out the things to sell."

'"Oh," said little Marika sadly.

'"Then you can go round and look at all the things there are to buy, but just look, mind, not buy."

'"Oh," said little Marika.

'"And then, at the end of the day, before we go home, you can choose something for yourself and I will give it to you as a present so you will always remember staying with me."

'"Oh!" said little Marika happily.

'All the farmers like old Marika had set up stalls to sell their vegetables and fruit and flowers.

'Little Marika worked hard to help her grandmother. Then old Marika said, "That's enough now. Off you go to look and choose!"

'Little Marika ran off gaily. She walked round the square looking in each shop window one by one.

'She looked at the baker's and at the sweet shop because she was hungry.

'"No," she said. "I won't buy a bun or a lollipop because if I eat them I will not have them to remind me of staying with old Marika. I will choose a toy, or a book or a pretty picture."

'But she could not find a toyshop or a bookshop or any pretty pictures. The town was very small, not like the big city where she lived with her parents which had shops of every kind you can imagine.

'Here there was just a grocer's shop and a shop full of string and buckets and brooms and a shop full of dull warm clothes for grown-ups and, at the last corner, a shoemaker's.

'She saw the shoemaker sitting near his window to catch the light.

'"I don't want a pair of shoes," she sighed, "or a bucket, or a bag of flour, or a bun or a lollipop." And she began to turn away sadly. But what was the shoemaker doing? He wasn't making shoes. He wasn't mending shoes. He was carving something out of a piece of wood and, by the shape of his mouth, she could see he was whistling. He looked up and smiled at her and held up a little wooden cat.

'"Oh!" cried little Marika. "That's it. That's what I want!"

'And she flew back to old Marika and tugged at her hand.

'"I've found it!" she said. "I've found the very thing I want to remember you by."

'"Just a minute, just a minute!" laughed old Marika. "Can't you wait even a minute?"

'"No!" said little Marika and she dragged her grand-mother to the shoemaker's. And when she saw the little wooden cat she smiled and said, "Now that's nice," and took out a big coin from her purse and paid the shoe-maker and gave Marika the little wooden cat and a big fat kiss.'

'And then they went home,' put in Marika.

'Yes,' said Grannie.

'And little Marika's mother and father soon came and fetched her and she went back with them to the big city. With the little wooden cat.'

She sighed happily. 'I love that story,' she said.

'Ahh,' said her grannie. 'But it's not quite the end.'

'Is there a bit I don't know?' asked Marika.

'Oh yes,' said Grannie. 'You never asked so I never told you: how does the little wooden cat come to be in my glass cabinet?'

'No!' said Marika. 'I never did ask, did I? How did you get it?'

'Well,' said Grannie. 'When that little Marika was about ten there was a war in her country and she had to run away with her mother and father and come to this country to be safe.'

'Oh,' said Marika. 'How terrible.'

'Yes,' said her grannie. 'They had to leave in a hurry, but before they left, little Marika's mother said to her "You can bring one small thing which you couldn't bear to leave behind." And, of course, she chose . . .'

'The little wooden cat,' said Marika.

'Yes,' said Grannie. 'And when I was about your age she gave it to me.'

'And did she tell you the story too?'

'Of course,' said Grannie.

'And was it your favourite story?'

'Of course,' said Grannie. 'But even that's not quite the end.'

And she got up and went to the glass cabinet and opened the door.

'Here you are, Marika. Now you take the little wooden cat home with you and perhaps one day you can tell the story to another little Marika . . .'

'Who will tell it to another little Marika,' said Marika sleepily, 'and she will tell it to another little Marika and on and on and on . . . so it will always be Marika's favourite story.'

Patrick by Parcel

Alexander McCall Smith

Every year, on his birthday, Patrick got presents by parcel. There would be a knock on the door, and there, standing on the doorstep, would be the postman.

'Parcels for you again, Patrick,' he would say. 'Is it your birthday today?'

'Yes,' Patrick would reply. And then, taking the parcels, he would say: 'Thank you very much.'

The parcels always came from the same places. There would be one from his uncle, who lived in their town but who liked to send presents by post anyway, and there would be one from his aunt in Australia. Then there would be a third, from Patrick's grandmother, who lived in Ireland and who usually sent him the same thing every year – two pairs of green socks.

Patrick enjoyed opening his parcels. He would cut the stamps off the wrapping paper and roll the string into a ball. Then he would neatly fold the paper and put it away in a cupboard until he could find a use for it.

Then, just after his sixth birthday, a very strange idea came into Patrick's head.

'I wish I were a parcel,' he said to himself. 'Then I could send myself off somewhere – just like that. It would be such fun.'

And then he thought again: 'Why shouldn't I be a parcel after all? I can wrap myself up in brown paper, stick a stamp on the outside, and post myself at the Post Office.'

It all seemed very simple and, after a few moments' further thought, Patrick had made up his mind. He had always longed to visit his aunt in Australia, and this seemed to be the ideal way to do it. She had sent him a parcel for his birthday, and now it was time for him to send her one in return. The only difference would be that he would be in the parcel which she received, and what a surprise that would be for her!

That afternoon Patrick bought some brown wrapping paper – the strongest they had in the shop – and then he bought some string. Shutting himself in his room, he wrapped himself up in the paper, carefully leaving two holes for his arms to stick out of, and then wrote his aunt's address on the outside. Next, all parcelled up, he hopped out of the house and made his way down to the Post Office. There he paid for some stamps – getting some very funny looks from the woman behind the counter – and, before anybody could say anything, he posted himself through the letter box.

'Well, well!' said the postman as he saw the strange parcel arrive on his desk. 'This parcel looks remarkably like a wrapped-up boy!'

But of course there was no reason why wrapped up boys should not go by post, and so he stamped Patrick on the nose with his big rubber stamp and popped him into the van, along with all the other parcels.

It felt very strange being a parcel. Patrick was lifted up and then put down again. Somebody shook him a little, and then put him on a conveyor belt. Then he was taken off and put in a pile with other parcels. Some of these were soft; some were hard. Some squeaked when he pressed them; others bounced. Patrick couldn't see any of the other parcels, but he knew they were there. One of them barked at him when he touched it, and Patrick knew that somebody had put a dog in the post.

Soon Patrick heard a loud noise and felt the floor swaying beneath him. Together with a lot of other parcels, he was lifted up into the air and loaded into a hold. Not long after that there came the sound of a door slamming, followed by a tremendous roar. Patrick realized that he was on a plane and that he would soon take off.

'It's worked!' he said out loud. 'I'm really on my way to Australia!'

It was not a comfortable journey. Upstairs, in the passenger compartment, the passengers all drank orange juice, took their shoes off, read magazines, and ate meals off little plastic trays. Down below, with all the parcels and the suitcases, Patrick was squashed and buffeted, and he soon felt quite ill. At last, though, the journey came to an end, and with a bump they landed in Australia. All the passengers got out and stretched in the bright, warm air. Patrick waited with the other parcels until a truck drove up and they were unloaded.

'That's an odd-looking one,' he heard the truck driver say. 'Looks a bit like a boy from here!'

At the post office, Patrick was taken out of the van and placed on a long table. This was where the parcels were sorted and given to the postmen. Patrick was handed to his postman, who grunted from the weight as he lifted him into his van.

'I can't imagine what's in here,' the postman said. 'It's certainly very heavy,'

'I'm in here,' Patrick muttered. 'And I wish you'd not waste any more time and deliver me!'

'What was that?' said the postman. 'Surely that parcel didn't speak to me!'

'No,' said Patrick, quite loudly this time. 'You just imagined it.'

'Oh,' said the postman. 'I see.'

By the time he was delivered to his aunt's house, Patrick had had enough of being a parcel. With great relief he felt his aunt tearing at the wrapping paper. Then, with a cry of welcome, out leapt Patrick.

'Patrick!' shouted his aunt. 'What a wonderful present!'

Patrick and his aunt sat down to tea without any further delay. Aftr his long journey, Patrick was pleased to have something to eat and drink, and it was only after he had eaten three cakes that he began to tell his aunt all about his trip. She laughed when he told her about the parcel which barked, and she shook her head when he mentioned how uncomfortable he had been in the plane.

'I've never been anywhere by parcel,' she said. 'But I can just imagine how uncomfortable it must be!'

Patrick spent the next week with his aunt. She showed him all the sights he had longed to see. He saw great white beaches and tall forests of eucalyptus trees. They visited a farm where there were some kangaroos and thousands and thousands of sheep. They saw a koala bear in a tree and a man throwing a boomerang in the air. Australia was just as Patrick had imagined it, and even more exciting than that!

Finally, Patrick's aunt thought that it was time for him to go home.

'You can come and see me again next year,' she said. 'I'll think of many more things for us to do.'

'I'd love to come,' Patrick said. 'I shall start saving up for the stamps the moment I get back.'

Patrick's aunt laughed.

'I don't think you should come by parcel again,' she said. 'It would be far better for you to come properly – as a passenger in the plane. I shall send you the ticket myself.'

They walked to the Post Office the next day. There, Patrick's aunt wrapped him up carefully in a special padded wrapping paper she had bought and wrote his address on the outside.

'You'll be far more comfortable in this sort of wrapping paper,' she said to him. 'And you also have those sandwiches and drinks I packed for you.'

Then Patrick's aunt kissed the parcel where she thought its cheek might be, and popped it into the post.

When the postman staggered up the path with the unwieldy parcel, Patrick's parents had no idea what he might be bringing. They had heard from Patrick's aunt that Patrick was in Australia, and so they had not been too worried about him, but they had not expected to find him coming back quite so soon.

'Patrick!' shouted his mother as she unwrapped the parcel. 'So you're back – and just in time for tea.'

Patrick climbed out of the wrapping paper and stretched his arms.

'That parcel was a bit more comfortable,' he said. 'But I don't think I'll travel by parcel again. At least, not for some time.'

'Would you like to keep the stamps?' Patrick's mother asked. 'You normally do.'

'Yes,' said Patrick. 'I think I will. I don't have any Australian stamps quite like those ones, and they'll remind me of my holiday.'

Patrick stuck the Australian stamps in his album, and each time he looked at them after that he smiled.

'Yes,' he would say to himself. 'It's true. I really did go by parcel!'

Just Once

Alison Morgan

Tina stirred in her sleep. She was warm and comfortable, curled up in her basket, a fat little oatmeal-coloured puppy just coming up to her two-months birthday.

One eye began to open, just a crack. Then she was out of her basket in an instant, her front teeth wide apart, tail up, hair bristling all down her back, eyes wide, and barking her head off.

A great bright white torch was shining straight in through the window.

There were footsteps above, and an angry voice shouted, 'Be quiet, Tina!'

Tina stared at the bright white torch and barked again. She could not help it. Steps came thumping down the stairs.

Tina's tail began to wag very fast when she heard him come into the room, but she did not take her eyes off the torch.

'Silly puppy,' he said. 'It's only the moon.' He drew the curtains across to shut out the bright white light.

Tina ran to him and wriggled all round his legs to

show how pleased she was that he had got up in the middle of the night to come and talk to her.

'Basket,' he said, pointing. 'Go to sleep.' And he went back upstairs, shutting the door behind him.

Tina lay down and closed her eyes. 'Only the moon,' she said. 'What's the moon?' she wondered. 'Is it still there, behind the curtain?' One eye opened again. There was definitely a pale light shining through the curtain.

Tina got up and gave the curtain a tug, and shook it. She began to swing it to and fro, growling fiercely.

'Be quiet,' said Cat's voice, from somewhere above Tina. He sounded sleepy, and was not purring.

'There's a Moon out there,' said Tina, 'and it's trying to get in!'

'Moon, eh?' said Cat. A black shadow on top of the radiator rolled down the side and turned itself into an upright sitting Cat on the carpet beside Tina. Tina had pulled the curtain so that a slice of light shone on the carpet and on the two shining eyes of Cat.

Cat jumped onto an armchair and then onto the window-sill, pushing the curtain wider open.

'There it is!' cried Tina. 'It's a Moon!'

Cat paid no attention. He stared out, not at the moon, but down into the garden.

Tina jumped up into the chair and put her front feet on the window-sill. The moon had moved away from the window and was lighting all the garden in silver and grey.

'What is a Moon?' she asked.

Cat did not answer, but jumped onto the floor and walked towards the kitchen. Tina tumbled off the chair and ran after him.

'Where are you going?' she asked.

'Out,' said Cat. He walked to the closed back door, made a clattering noise, and disappeared.

Tina stared around the dark kitchen. One moment Cat was there, the next he wasn't. She crept right up to the back door, sniffing hard. When she touched the door with her nose, it moved; Tina was so surprised that she jumped back. That was when the door swung back and batted her.

She sat down and looked at the door. Then she tried again, and again the door batted her on the nose.

Puzzled, she trotted back into the living-room, jumped onto the armchair, put her feet on the window-sill, and peered out.

The moon still hung above the garden. By its light, Tina saw Cat, Cat out in the garden, Cat creeping over the lawn, one slow foot after another, staring ahead at a rough patch of grass.

Tina tumbled off the armchair again and ran through to the kitchen. If Cat could disappear through a door, so could she. She took a run at the swinging bit of the door; there was a clattering noise, and Tina was out in the silver-grey garden.

Or at least, not quite. Her head was out, and her front paws, but her fat tummy filled the cat-flap more tightly than Cat did, and her hind legs scrabbled on the tiled kitchen floor in vain. She gave a doleful wail.

Cat strolled round the corner and sat down facing her, curling his tail neatly round his toes. 'Too fat,' he remarked.

'What shall I do?' panted Tina.

Cat got up. 'Chase me!' he said, and shot away across the garden in a wild curve, tail on one side, and ran half-way up a tree.

Tina popped out of the cat-flap like a cork out of a bottle and went pounding after him. By the time she reached the foot of the tree, Cat was lying on a branch half-way to the moon.

'When I'm bigger,' said Tina, 'I'll climb all the trees in the garden. To the very top.'

Cat laughed, walked along the branch till it began to dip, dropped silently to the ground and raced off on another wild zig-zag – and was gone.

Tina started to bounce after him, but a leaf fluttered down and she tried to catch it. Then she saw a silvery earthworm, and nudged it with her nose. The worm coiled itself into knots with surprise, and Tina was surprised, too. She backed away and watched from a safe distance, under a garden seat.

As she watched, a small surprising person trotted fast across the lawn, sharp nose heading straight for the worm. A gulp and a swallow, and the worm was gone. The sharp-nosed person looked up and two beady black eyes stared intently at the garden seat.

'Smells like Dog,' muttered the person. 'Looks like a striped cushion.'

'I'm *not* a striped cushion!' said Tina, and trotted out from under the seat, leaving the striped shadows on the grass.

The person promptly turned into a perfect round ball.

Tina drew back. First, a Cat that disappeared. Then a worm that turned into a spring, and disappeared. Now a person that turned into a ball – would that disappear, too?

Tina crept forward, sniffing. The ball did not disappear. It pricked her nose.

'Ow!' cried Tina, and ran away.

When she had put the whole length of the garden between her and the prickly ball, she turned round. The ball was slowly uncurling itself until it had a dark pointed face at one end and four short legs like castors. Then it trotted briskly back the way it had come.

Cat dropped out of the sky and landed beside Tina. 'Hedgehog,' he said, and jumped up onto a gate that led into a field.

Tina tried to get between the bars of the gate, but couldn't. Then she tried under the gate, and could, just. She galloped away across the field looking for Cat, and blundered into a large pale lump sitting in a pool of black shadow. It was soft, and had a warm, greasy smell.

'Baa!' said the lump, and scrambled to its feet.

Suddenly the whole field was full of pale lumps baa-ing. Sheep! When they saw it was only a small puppy that had disturbed their sleep they all started to run towards her, baa-ing like mad. Tina fled.

She ran and ran until she found she was in a farmyard. Barns and sheds cast dark shadows along three sides, and a house with windows glittered in the moonlight on the fourth. All was silent. The yard was full of interesting smells of animals and people and hay and diesel, and Tina trotted about sniffing excitedly. She found a mountain of mucky straw in one corner, and climbed up in it. Oh, what a lovely smell! She lay on her back and rolled in it till she tumbled off.

She saw some biscuit-like things scattered on the yard.

'I'm hungry,' she thought, and began to gobble them down.

'Leave it!' snarled a hoarse, fierce voice, and Tina spun round, trembling. From under a door gleamed a set of sharp white teeth, bared between curling lips.

'Oh!' said Tina, and she put her head down between her paws and wagged her tail, to say she was sorry. She could see now that the teeth belonged to a sheepdog, poking its head through a ragged hole in the bottom of a barn door.

'Come over here,' said the sheepdog, looking more friendly. Tina crept closer, on her tummy, to show

respect; but she kept out of reach of the sharp teeth.

'What are you doing here?' asked the sheepdog.

Tina explained about the moon and the sheep.

'Ah,' said the sheepdog. 'Last night out, eh?'

'No,' said Tina. 'First night out.'

'Could be the same thing,' said the sheepdog. 'How did you get out?'

Tina told him about the cat-flap and the Cat.

'Just so,' said the sheepdog. 'I got out once, when I was your age, through this hole. Come on in, and I'll tell you about it.'

He backed away, and Tina crept up to the hole and looked in. The moon shone through a high window and made a square of light on the floor, lighting up part of a tractor, a pitchfork, a heap of clean straw and the sheepdog, standing up and waving a feathery tail. She crawled through, nervously. The waving tail made her feel friendly, but she was not at all sure about the sharp white teeth.

'I won't eat you,' said the sheepdog, and he bent his head and touched Tina's snub nose with his pointed one.

They sniffed a greeting and after that Tina felt safe, and wiggled all over with relief.

'Now lie down and listen,' said the sheepdog. 'When I was a puppy, I put my head out through that hole, and saw the moon shining. So I crept out without waking my mother and sisters, and ran all over the yard and out into the fields. There I found a sheeprack with a whole lot of sheepnuts in it, like the ones you were eating just now – and I ate them all. Afterwards I felt so fat and full I lay down and went to sleep.

'But the clouds came up and covered the moon, and I was woken by rain beating down on me. I was cold and wet through, and feeling sick because of so many sheep-nuts inside me. It was pitch dark and I took a long time to find the barn.

'But worst of all, when I did find it, I couldn't get through the hole. I had eaten too much! My mother woke up, but there was nothing she could do, and for the rest of the night I sat outside in the pouring rain. I howled

60

and I howled, but nobody heard me until the farmer got up to milk the cows. Oh, I was so glad to see him!'

'What did he do?'

'Oh, he laughed, and said, "You poor little pup!" and took me in to Mrs Farmer, who rubbed me dry and put me down in front of the fire till I had stopped shivering; then I went back to my mum.'

'You never went out at night again?'

'I couldn't. I was too big to get through the hole. But I'm glad I did it, just that once, because now I know what it's like out there, when the moon shines bright.'

He peered through the hole. 'You'd best be off. There's a black cloud coming up.'

Tina had been dozing off in the straw, but she suddenly remembered the garden gate and the cat-flap. How many sheepnuts had she eaten before the sheepdog stopped her?

'Goodbye,' she said. 'Thank you for having me.'

'I expect we'll meet again,' said the sheepdog. 'In the daytime.'

Tina squeezed through the hole, tumbled through the farm gate, galloped across the field, taking care not to wake up the sleeping sheep, and flattened herself in the mud under the garden gate. She rushed up to the cat-flap and pushed it with her nose.

It wouldn't open.

'Let me,' said Cat's voice in her ear. He stood up against the door on his hind legs and with one paw, instead of pushing the flap, he lifted it towards him. A dim orange glow from the radiator lit up the square hole.

Tina rushed at it – and stuck, half-way through.

'Help!' she cried.

'Ah,' said Cat. He arched his back and fluffed out his tail, and let out the most horrible fiendish yowl you ever did hear. It catapulted Tina through the hole, across the kitchen floor and into her basket in a trice.

Upstairs, a window was flung open and an angry voice

shouted. But Cat was already settling down on the radiator.

'Oh, thank you,' said Tina.

'*I* didn't want to stay out all night,' said Cat. 'It looked like rain.'

'I'll never, never do it again,' said Tina.

'No, I don't suppose you will,' said Cat. 'My goodness, how you smell. I wonder what They will say in the morning.'

Tina was almost asleep. 'I'm glad I did it,' she said. 'Just once.'

The Bomakle

Andrew Matthews

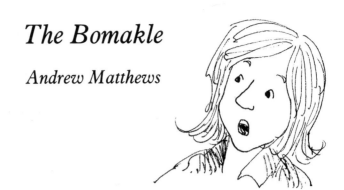

Wayne was a horrible little boy. He chased cats around his back garden with a stick. He poked out his tongue at old people when he passed them in the street. Instead of speaking in a normal voice and asking for things politely, Wayne would shout:

'Buy me some sweets or I'll scream until I'm sick!'

Wayne's mother and father didn't know what to do. They were such kind people that they couldn't punish their son, even though he made their lives a misery. If Wayne didn't like the food that was cooked for him, he threw the plate on to the floor. If his parents bought him clothes that he didn't like, he would throw them out of the bedroom window. One Christmas, when Wayne opened a present from his Aunt Rosie and saw that it was a set of handkerchiefs with the letter 'W' on one corner, he was so cross that he pushed over the Christmas tree.

Not surprisingly, Wayne had no friends. The children who lived on his street wouldn't play with him. At school he was bossy, rough and rude and the other children didn't like him one bit – nor did the teachers.

One rainy Saturday morning, while Wayne's mother and father were shopping in the supermarket, Wayne played a game in the rain outside. He found the deepest, dirtiest puddle and when anyone walked near he jumped right into the middle, kicking his wellingtons about. Seeing other people soaked with muddy rain-water made Wayne snigger.

He had soaked a lot of people that morning, when he noticed a little old lady coming out of the supermarket carrying a heavy bag of shopping. She was a round little old lady with snowy white hair and blue spectacles. Wayne smiled to himself, because she was just the sort of person he most enjoyed splashing. He waited until she got right up to the puddle and then – KER-DUNK! – he jumped in.

But when Wayne looked at the old lady, he was surprised to see that she wasn't upset or angry with him.

'That wasn't very nice, was it?' she asked gently.

'I'm Wayne!' shouted Wayne. 'I'm not very nice. I'm horrible! Your face looks like a pig's bottom! I'm going to be a battle when I grow up!'

'You can't be a battle on your own!' frowned the old lady.

'I can!' bawled Wayne.

'Well, Wayne,' said the old lady, wiping a drip of dirty water from the tip of her nose, 'I'm afraid to say that if you don't mend your ways and start behaving yourself, the Bomakle will come for you.'

'The what?' asked Wayne.

'The Bomakle,' repeated the old lady. 'And you know what will happen to you then, don't you?'

'What?' said Wayne.

'You'll be discumnoculated.'

'What's that?' snapped Wayne.

'It's what happens to children who are especially horrible.'

'It'll happen to me, then!' said Wayne proudly. 'I'm the most especially horrible boy in the world!'

'You may be right,' sighed the old lady sadly as she walked off into the rain. 'You can expect the Bomakle any day now.'

'You're bonkers!' Wayne called after her.

66

That night, Wayne was worse than ever. He tipped strawberry yoghurt over the electric cooker and ran round the house shaking up cans of fizzy drink so that sticky foam went whooshing out all over the place. At tea-time he poured half a bottle of tomato sauce over his fish fingers, then dipped a chip into the sauce and wrote his name on the table-cloth.

Just then came the most tremendous hammering on the front door. It made the house shake.

'Whoever can that be?' said Wayne's mother.

'I'd better go and see,' said Father.

Before he could get out of the chair there was a splintering crash followed by a loud bang, and a mysterious stranger burst into the dining room.

It was a gigantic hairy
man, as round as he was
tall. He was dressed in
black clothes and a red
cloak. A helmet with horns
sat on top of his head.
In his left hand he
carried a thick stick
covered with silver bells
that jingled when he walked.

'Who are you?' gasped Father.

'I am the Bomakle!' cried the stranger. His voice was
so loud that all the pictures fell off the walls. 'I've come
for your boy! He must be discumnoculated at once!'

'Discumnoculated?' exclaimed Mother, bursting into
tears.

'There, there, dear!' said Father. 'I'm sure it will all be
for the best!'

68

The Bomakle looked straight at Wayne with eyes as red as the inside of a volcano.

'Let's go, boy!' he roared. 'Don't bother to pack. You won't need pyjamas where you're going!'

'Buzz off, furry chops!' yelled Wayne. 'I haven't finished my tea yet!'

The Bomakle jumped across the room, grabbed Wayne by the scruff of the neck, lifted him out of his chair and kept him dangling in the air. Wayne struggled and kicked, but it was no use.

'I'll be off then,' said the Bomakle. 'Sorry about smashing your front door down. I was in a hurry.'

'That's quite all right,' said Father. 'I'll mend it after tea. There's nothing worth watching on television, so it will give me something to do.'

The Bomakle carried Wayne outside. The evening sky was filled with black clouds and a strong wind was blowing.

'Where are you taking me?' shouted Wayne.

'To Scotland,' replied the Bomakle. 'I've got a lair in the Highlands. It's a filthy, miserable hovel. I love it!'

And with that, the Bomakle took a mighty leap into the sky. He went up for thousands and thousands of feet and then started to come down again. Wayne looked at all the tiny roads and houses below and felt ill.

The Bomakle landed in a field a hundred miles from Wayne's house and jumped up again. He went straight into the middle of a storm cloud. Thunder rumbled all around. Wayne was pelted with hailstones the size of peas. A crooked streak of lightning hit the Bomakle on top of the head and made steam shoot out from his beard.

'That tickles!' chuckled the Bomakle.

In no time at all, they were in Scotland. The Bomakle's lair was a huge old shed made of rusty iron. It was on

top of a mountain that was so high the snow on the ground never melted. Wayne shivered with the cold. The Bomakle trudged through the snow, whistling cheerfully.

The door of the shed creaked open, and there stood a grubby hag, wearing grey rags. Her hair hung down in greasy strands. She was cross-eyed and the tip of her nose almost touched the point of her chin.

'Who's that you've got with you?' she screamed in a voice like a knife squeaking on a plate.

'This is Wayne!' answered the Bomakle.

'Are we going to roast him or stew him?' asked the hag, licking her lips.

'We're going to discumnoculate him,' said the Bomakle.

'What larks!' cackled the hag.

The inside of the Bomakle's lair was awful. The only furniture was wooden crates, covered with dirty sacks. The walls and floor were the colour of cow-pat. In one corner a big iron pot hung over a log fire and filled the shed with a strange smell.

The Bomakle dropped Wayne on to one of the crates, where he hugged himself and shivered and wished that he could be at home in his nice, warm bed.

'The boy must be hungry!' cried the Bomakle. 'I took him away in the middle of his tea!'

'Then I'll get him some supper!' screeched the hag.

'Do you two *have* to shout all the time?' grumbled Wayne. 'You're starting to give me a headache!'

'Hah!' boomed the Bomakle. 'And many's the head-ache you must have given your poor dear mother with *your* shouting! Well, now you know what it feels like, don't you, boy?'

The hag took a wooden bowl, hobbled over to the iron pot and filled it with a spoon. She placed the bowl and spoon on the crate beside Wayne.

'What's this?' cried Wayne. 'It looks and smells horrible!'

'Try some!' said the hag. 'You'll find it doesn't taste as bad as it looks and smells.'

Wayne took a spoonful, blew on it to cool it down and then took a big slurp.

It tasted like old leaves, slug slime and green mould.

'Y-U-U-K!' spluttered Wayne. 'I thought you said it didn't taste as bad as it looks and smells.'

'It doesn't!' laughed the hag. 'It tastes worse!'

'Do you know what's in that pot, boy?' the Bomakle asked sternly.

'N-no!' stammered Wayne.

'Every scrap of every meal you've ever thrown on the floor!' said the Bomakle. He pointed to an enormous bucket standing by the door. 'And now I'm going to throw ice-cold puddle water all over you.'

'No!' shouted Wayne. 'I won't let you!'

He jumped to his feet and began to run round the shed. The Bomakle followed him, waving the stick with bells on.

'And this is how the cats in your back garden feel!' he bellowed.

Wayne was trying so hard to stay out of the way of the stick that he forgot all about the hag. She jumped in front of him and tipped the bucket of water over his head.

Wayne was frozen into an icicle. The water ran down into his socks and made them squelchy.

It was too much for Wayne. He sat down on the wet floor and cried and cried. The hot tears made clean streaks in the dirt on his face.

'What's the matter?' asked the Bomakle. 'Don't you want to stay here and eat our food and play games with us?'

'No!' sobbed Wayne. 'I want to go home. I want to hug my mum and dad and have a mug of hot chocolate and a biscuit. I'm never going to shout at them again! And I'm going to eat every bit of every meal I'm given!'

'Even spinach?' asked the hag.

'Yes!' snuffled Wayne. 'And I'm going to stop splashing people. It's awful to be splashed! And I'm not going to chase cats any more, I'm going to make friends with them.'

'They like to be scratched behind their ears,' said the Bomakle. 'But do it gently, mind!'

'Please, Mr Bomakle,' said Wayne very politely, 'will you take me home now?'

The Bomakle looked closely at Wayne and smiled. His teeth were like old park railings.

'Yes!' he said. 'I reckon you've been discumnoculated good and proper!'

And it was true. When Wayne arrived home, not long after his father had finished mending the front door, he was a different little boy. He was polite, kind, gentle and quiet, and he was never, ever horrible again.

Well . . . not often, anyway.

Fleabag

Jacqueline Wilson

Molly woke up very early on Sunday. She slipped out of her bunk bed and peered at her big sister Susan in the top bunk. Susan was fast asleep. She stayed asleep even when Molly tickled her neck and tugged her toes. Susan was never any fun in the early morning.

Baby Simon in the next door bedroom would wake up willingly enough, but he wasn't any fun either. He never wanted to play. He'd just roar for his bottle. He didn't have much time for anything but his bottle. He didn't even seem to like his blue teddy bear. Gran had given Simon the bear when he was born. Molly thought it was a waste of a present because Simon was much too young to play with it properly. Molly had tried to sneak the blue teddy into her own toy cupboard but Mum made her put him back into Simon's cot.

Mum and Dad were still fast asleep too. Molly didn't have to peep round their door to check. She could hear snoring.

She went downstairs by herself and made her breakfast. She wasn't allowed to touch the kettle or the cooker but she didn't need to. She went to the fridge and poured herself a glass of milk without spilling any. (Well, just a drop or two, but they were soon mopped up.) Then she set about making herself a sandwich. She couldn't decide whether she wanted a raspberry jam sandwich or a banana sandwich. In the end she decided to try a raspberry jam *and* banana sandwich and it tasted delicious.

Then she went into the living-room and played a cartoon on the video. She curled up on the sofa to watch it. It didn't seem quite so funny watching it by herself. She wished she had someone for company. Even a teddy.

She nipped upstairs. She could peep into Simon's room and see if he was awake. If he was still asleep he wouldn't really miss his teddy, would he?

'Hello, Molly!'

It was Mum.

'Are you after Simon's teddy again?' Mum whispered.

'I was just sort of looking at him,' Molly whispered back.

'Let's go downstairs. Simon's still fast asleep. We'll leave him alone, eh? *And* his teddy,' said Mum. 'You're up early, Molly.'

'So are you, Mum,' said Molly.

'Yes, I'm going to go to the Car Boot Sale down at the school.' Mum looked at Molly. 'Do you fancy coming with me?'

Molly nodded, pleased, though she wasn't very sure what a Car Boot Sale was. Mum made a cup of tea and Molly made some more sandwiches and enjoyed another breakfast. Then they got washed and dressed. Simon and Susan and Dad were still fast asleep.

'They can look after each other,' said Mum. 'It'll make a change. I'll leave Dad a note. Now, it's cold out. Better wrap up warm.'

Mum made Molly wear the pink woolly hat and scarf Gran had knitted for her. Molly worried she might look like a baby.

'I don't like pink,' Molly moaned.

'Better than going blue with cold,' said Mum. 'Come on, Molly. We don't want to miss the bargains, do we?'

The school wasn't very far away so Mum didn't bother to drive.

'Don't you need a car at a Car Boot Sale?' asked Molly.

'No, not if you're just looking round. People turn their cars into little shops and sell all their old bits and pieces. You'll see,' said Mum.

Molly did see when they got to the Car Boot Sale. There were lots of cars parked all the way round the big playground. People had spread out their things for sale. All sorts of things. Broken televisions, biscuit tins, binoculars. Sideboards and saucers and great heaps of shoes. Old records, old books, old toys.

'Ooh, look at that fire engine!' said Molly. 'Ooh, look at that baby doll. Ooh, look at those roller skates. Oh, Mum, can I have the fire engine? And the baby doll? And the roller skates?'

'The fire engine has lost a wheel and it's ever so expensive anyway. The baby doll has got funny eyes. And you're not big enough for roller skates just yet,' said Mum. 'Let's have a look at these records. Oh, this was a hit when I was a teenager. I haven't heard it for ages. Look at these books, Molly. There's that annual Susan was wanting, and it's only 10p.'

'Come on, Mum, let's see some more toys,' Molly begged.

There weren't that many toy stalls. Molly started to get sick of all the junk stalls and dragged her feet and pulled at her silly pink hat.

'Let's go home now, Mum, this is getting boring,' Molly whined – and then she stood still, staring. She'd spotted something in the very end car boot. Not something. Someone.

It was a big teddy bear with honey coloured fur, rather rubbed. One of his ears was hanging by a thread and his nose looked as if it had been bitten at some stage. But he had all four paws and a big smile on his face. He seemed to be smiling straight at Molly.

'Mum! Oh, Mum, look at that teddy,' Molly said, tugging at Mum.

'Mmm? Oh yes, he's nice,' said Mum vaguely, not even looking. 'Right. Have you had enough then? We'd better go and see how Dad's coping with Simon.'

'Mum! The teddy!' Molly said urgently.

'Which one? That grubby old teddy over there?'

'Mum, please please please can I have that teddy?'

'No, Molly, of course you can't. Look. He's all coming to bits. He's far too tattered. You don't want that nasty old bear.'

'I do,' said Molly.

'No, come on, lovie. We've got the annual for Susan. We'll look for a good book for you too – and then we'll go home.'

'I want the teddy,' said Molly, and she sidled over to him and held his paw. He seemed to be holding tightly back.

'Molly! Don't be naughty. Look, you've got heaps of cuddly toys at home.'

'I haven't got a teddy.'

'Well. Maybe you can have Simon's teddy after all,' said Mum. 'He's not old enough to make a fuss about it.'

But Molly shook her head.

'I don't want Simon's teddy. I want my teddy. This teddy. Oh, Mum, please.'

'He'll probably be too dear. People charge a fortune for these old teddies,' said Mum, but when she asked the price it was cheaper than she'd expected.

'Please!' Molly said again, hugging the teddy hard to her chest.

'Oh all right,' said Mum, sighing.

'Oh, Mum, thank you ever so much! Oh he's lovely!' said Molly, kissing him all over his ragged face.

'Don't do that! He might be all germy. Come on. I'm going to nip back to the record stall. I might as well have a present too.'

Molly hugged her teddy all the way home, her face pink with happiness so that she matched her woolly hat.

Dad was cross when they got in the front door.

'You might have given me some warning! Simon's been yelling his head off and he won't take his bottle properly. Susan can't do her Maths homework. I can't find the potato peeler. I don't know how long the chicken takes to  cook and Gran's coming to lunch, remember? And what on earth is Molly holding? Throw that filthy old fleabag in the dustbin!'

'He's my teddy!' said Molly indignantly.

'Calm down, love,' said Mum. 'I'll give Simon his bottle. And I'm quite good at Maths. I never use a peeler, I use a little knife. We'll get the chicken on in good time. And I know Molly's teddy is an old fleabag but she seems to love him.'

Dad calmed down a little. But he still glared at Molly's teddy.

'No, you can't have it, Molly. Mum shouldn't have bought it for you. It could really have fleas inside it.'

'Yuck!' said Susan. 'Throw it away, Molly.'

'I can't. He's mine,' said Molly. 'I don't mind him being a Fleabag.'

'Don't be silly, Molly. Here, he's going out now and

that's an end of it,' said Dad, snatching the teddy.

Molly started screaming. She was still crying when Gran came round.

'What's the matter with my little Molly?' Gran said, giving her a cuddle.

'Dad won't let me have my Fleabag,' Molly wept.

'Won't he?' said Gran. 'What's your Fleabag, pet?'

Molly took Gran to see poor Fleabag who had been put outside the kitchen door, right next to the dustbin.

'Oh, he's an old teddy!' said Gran. 'Your dad had one just like him when he was a little boy. Ever so dirty and tattered.'

'Dad!' said Molly, outraged.

'Well, it was *our* dirt,' said Dad. 'We don't know what this Fleabag is infested with.'

'Why don't you give him the freezer treatment?' said Gran. 'That'll cure him of anything. You know.'

They didn't know, so Gran told them.

'You put the teddy into a big plastic bag and tie it up tight. Then you put it in the freezer for twenty-four hours. That's enough to freeze up any old fleas. Then he can come out and Molly can play with him to her heart's content.'

It seemed an extraordinary idea.

'Plastic bags are dangerous. It would hurt him,' said Molly.

'They only hurt children. Your Fleabag is a teddy.'

'We don't want that old thing amongst all the frozen food,' said Dad.

'The plastic bag will be done up really tight. Nothing can get in or out.'

'Unless Fleabag bites his way through,' said Mum, giggling. 'We'd better watch out for paw marks in the butter.'

Gran found a big plastic bag and helped Molly wrap Fleabag inside. He didn't look too happy about the idea. He looked positively miserable when they'd crammed him into the freezer. Like a large wrapped chicken waiting to be cooked.

Dad still wasn't very pleased but Mum made him listen to her record and he started smiling and they did the funny sort of dance they used to do when they were teenagers. Then Mum helped Susan with her sums and Dad laid the table and Gran bounced baby Simon and his blue teddy on her knee. Molly stood beside the freezer. She pressed her nose to its cold side, whispering to Fleabag.

He had to stay in the freezer all Sunday afternoon. Molly begged for him to be taken out at night but Mum wouldn't hear of it. She wouldn't even let her take Fleabag out on Monday morning.

'Wait till you come home from school. Then we'll be really sure he's okay,' she said.

School seemed to last for ever and ever. But at last it was time to go home. Molly ran ahead of Mum and Susan and Simon in his pram. She ran straight into the kitchen, opened the freezer, and took Fleabag out of the cold into her warm arms. Mum insisted on unwrapping him, but after she'd given him a careful inspection she handed him over to Molly at last.

'My very own Fleabag,' said Molly. 'You poor boy. You're so very cold. You need to wrap up warm, pet.'

She got her pink woolly hat and scarf and tenderly dressed Fleabag in his new clothes. They suited him much more than Molly. He smiled and smiled.

When Dad came home from work he had a little box of chocolate animals. There were eight tiny chocolate teddies. Dad ate one. Mum ate one. They saved one for Gran. Baby Simon was too young to have any. Susan had two. Molly had two. And Fleabag had one all to himself.

Godsend the Convent Cat

Anne Rooke

'This is strange,' thought the kitten waking up and staring around. 'What am I doing here on this cold doorstep and – and where is my mother? Miaow – ow – ow.'

'What's all this noise?' asked Sister Agatha as she opened the convent door. 'And whatever was that?' she added as a grey ball of fluff hurtled past her down the hall and into the kitchen.

'Aar – aah,' yelled Sister Perpetua from the kitchen. 'A rat! There's a great rat in the kitchen,' and she slammed the kitchen door.

Sister Perpetua and Sister Agatha didn't know what to do, so they decided to tell Sister Lucy about the rat in the kitchen.

Now Sister Lucy was rather stern. She was in charge of the convent and she made sure that Sister Agatha and Sister Perpetua only did sensible things. The most sensible thing they did was to look after poor people who had no homes. The three sisters cooked food for these poor people and let them sleep in the front room and they prayed for them and worried about where the money was coming from. Well, Sister Lucy worried because she was in charge, but Sister Agatha and Sister Perpetua did not worry at all – until the kitten came.

'And how – ' said Sister Lucy when she bravely opened the kitchen door and found that Sister Perpetua's great rat was only a little cat, ' – and how are we going to spend our money feeding a cat when the poor people need all we can give them?'

'How indeed?' thought Sister Agatha and Sister Perpetua sadly as they looked at the kitten.

'No problem,' thought the kitten as she climbed into the bread bin. 'I'll look after myself.'

'Put it out at once,' said Sister Lucy. 'We cannot take in stray cats.'

So Sister Agatha gently picked up the kitten and pushed her back out of the front door. 'Go back home

and don't get run over,' she whispered.

But the kitten curled up on the doorstep and went to sleep in the sunshine.

Sometime later James arrived. He rang the convent's front door bell.

'Don't let the kitten in,' said Sister Agatha as she opened the door and the ball of grey fluff hurtled past her down to the kitchen again.

'Right you are,' said James. 'But is there any breakfast? And what's that rat doing in the margarine?'

'Oh no,' wailed Sister Agatha as she picked the kitten out of the margarine and shoved her out of the front door.

'Shoo, kitten. Go home. We can't have you,' she said.

The kitten licked her whiskers and scrambled up the wall to sit on a window-sill and carry on her snooze in the sunshine.

Meanwhile Sister Perpetua was cleaning the dining room. She swept around James eating his breakfast and around Old Veronica who was reading a newspaper. Then she opened the window to shake out her duster and – flop – the kitten fell inside.

'It wants to live here,' said James. 'But I will not have it climbing my trousers to eat my breakfast,' he added as he picked the kitten off his plate and dropped her back down on to the floor.

'And why not?' asked Old Veronica. 'Can't the poor creature have a scrap of food? Go on. Give it a bit.'

'Oh, very well then,' said James, giving the kitten a corner of bread and marge. And the kitten mewed and purred and tore into that bread and margarine.

'The poor creature's starving,' said James giving the kitten more. 'It needs a loving home. Here would do.'

'But we can't afford it,' wailed Sister Perpetua.

'Then it will have to earn its living,' said James.

'How?' asked Sister Perpetua.

'How?' thought the kitten pricking up its ears.

'Well now,' said James, thinking hard. 'Could it not pick the pockets of the rich? Just a thought,' he explained when he saw the look on Sister Perpetua's face. 'And of course it can always catch mice – or something,' he finished lamely.

But Sister Perpetua put the kitten out of the window again. 'Sorry, Puss,' she said.

That afternoon the kitten sat on the doorstep of the convent and watched the people going past. She sat up straight and stared at pockets. Quite a lot of pockets went past. Some had hands in them and some bulged – and they all seemed a very long way up.

But suddenly a bright red pair of trousers stopped beside the kitten. 'Hullo, Pussy,' said a boy's voice. 'What are you looking at?'

'Here goes,' thought the kitten and she launched herself into the air and clung with her sharp little claws to those red trousers.

'Hey!' shouted the boy as the kitten took a nose dive into the nearest pocket.

Down went the kitten into the dark. Wham – her nose hit something. She grabbed it in her teeth, tugged and somersaulted back up into the light. Then she fell backwards out of the pocket, twisted to land on her feet and sped off down the pathway at the side of the convent.

The boy straightened up and looked around, not sure what had hit him. He felt in his pocket and frowned. 'It's nicked my bubble gum,' he said.

The kitten sat by the back door of the convent and wagged her head and chewed. She spat and hissed and opened wide but she could not get that bubble gum out of her mouth.

'Whatever's the matter?' said Sister Lucy as she came out into the yard to go to the dustbin.

The kitten heaved a desperate and mighty sigh and disappeared behind an enormous bubble.

'Glory be!' said Sister Lucy. 'Sisters!' she called. 'Come quickly. That kitten! It's exploding!'

Sister Agatha and Sister Perpetua burst out of the convent and stopped dead, staring at the huge bubble. They looked at each other and Sister Agatha almost winked as she picked up the kitten and hooked out the bubble gum with her little finger. The kitten purred gratefully and looked around hopefully at the sisters. Were they pleased with the lump of gum, she wondered. It was difficult to tell.

'Put it down, Sister Agatha,' said Sister Lucy. But this time her voice was not quite so stern.

The kitten shook herself briskly and scuttled off back to the front of the convent. There was nothing to this pick-pocketing business, she decided. And she settled down to wait for her next victim.

She did not have long to wait. To her delight a pair of dark blue trousers stopped in front of her and, at the top of the trousers, were any number of huge pockets.

'Wow-ee,' thought the kitten and dashed up those trousers, dived under a flap and scuttled down deep into a big dark pocket. She burrowed about and found some-thing hard cold and slippery. She seized it in her teeth.

'Oy, oy,' said a deep voice as a hand came into the pocket after her. 'What's all this? Do I have a thief here?'

And the kitten, still clutching her find, was pulled out and plonked down – bump – in a policeman's helmet.

'Now listen to me, young cat,' said the policeman taking his whistle out of the kitten's mouth. 'No more of this thieving. It seems you are living with the good sisters here. And it would break their hearts if you turned out a thief. Do you understand?'

The kitten sat in that helmet and her whiskers drooped. She certainly did not want to break the sisters' hearts but how was a cat to earn a living?

And then she remembered James' words. Mouse catching. That was the answer.

Her tail went up and her whiskers hummed. She bounded out of the helmet and down the side path to the convent dustbin. The kitten had noticed an interesting smell around that dustbin and all cats are born knowing the smell of mice. She darted up to the dustbin and miaowed loudly. At once a startled mouse face dodged up over the rim of the dustbin.

'Excuse me,' the kitten whispered politely. 'May I catch you, please, to earn my living? We could just pretend if you would rather.'

'Why?' asked the mouse cleverly.

'So that I can stay and protect you from really nasty cats,' the kitten explained.

'It's a deal,' agreed the mouse.

When the sisters went into their chapel to pray that evening, Sister Lucy found the mouse lying on its back with its feet in the air and the kitten sitting proudly beside it.

'Good heavens!' said Sister Lucy and she carefully picked the mouse up by its tail. 'Aaaah – aaaah,' she added as the mouse whistled up her sleeve. 'It's alive!' she yelled. 'Get it off me – quick!'

Sister Agatha and Sister Perpetua jumped to her aid.

But the kitten was quicker. She shot up Sister Lucy's dress and on to her head. She scrambled around her collar and down inside her neck.

'Oi – quick,' the kitten whispered to the terrified mouse. 'Down the other sleeve. There's a hole in the corner by the door.' Then she scuttled around for a bit while the mouse made his get away.

When, at last, Sister Lucy grabbed the kitten and pulled her out of her dress, the little kitten began to purr. She shut her eyes and drummed like a vacuum cleaner. She fluffed up her hair like a bottle brush and went rigid with purring.

'I do believe that kitten loves you, Sister,' said Sister Agatha.

'I have never heard such a purr in a creature so young,'

added Sister Perpetua. ' 'Tis mortal sad that we cannot keep it when the mice eat so much good food.'

'Do they?' asked Sister Lucy sternly.

'Not yet,' said Sister Perpetua truthfully. 'But if they are in the house . . .'

Sister Lucy looked at the purring kitten in her hand. 'Then we need a cat,' she said firmly. 'And it might as well be this one. Perhaps, after all, it is a godsend.'

And from that day to this, Godsend, the convent cat, has never caught a mouse. She sits on the laps of the poor people who come to the convent. Sometimes she may help them eat their meals. But not very often. Mostly she just sits and purrs.

'That Godsend has made this convent into a home,' says Old Veronica contentedly.

'There's great comfort in a cat that just sits and purrs for its living,' says James.

'I am sure the mice would agree with that,' says Sister Lucy – sternly.

The Princess in the Mirror

Gordon Urquhart

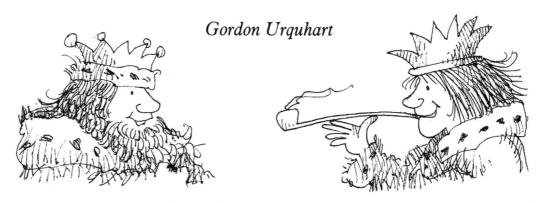

King Max and Queen Mo were the scruffiest king and queen in the whole world. King Max kept his socks in the kitchen sink. Queen Mo smoked a pipe the size of a saucepan. Their palace was never washed or dusted or scrubbed. It was a tip.

One summer's day, Queen Mo gave birth to a baby daughter with chubby cheeks.

'Do I have to wash for the christening party?' asked King Max.

'Of course not,' said Queen Mo. 'We'll just have a little gathering with friends. No dukes or countesses.'

'No fairy godmothers, either,' King Max decided. 'They're too fussy about dust.'

The baby princess was christened Rosamunda, Rosie for short. After the ceremony, King Max and Queen Mo invited their relatives to tea. They ate fruit cake and drank lemonade. Then they played musical chairs and pass-the-parcel twice. Queen Mo won every game –

except the egg-and-spoon race, because she was too fat
to run.

'I suppose I should start clearing up,' said Queen Mo
at the end of the party, looking round at the mess.

Suddenly there was a terrific bang. A nasty face
appeared at the window.

'Oh, dear,' gasped Queen Mo. 'It's a wicked fairy.'

The fairy flew into the room. She was tall, with long
green hair and flashing eyes. A cruel smile played on her
purple lips.

'We're sorry we didn't invite you to the party,' stammered Queen Mo. 'Please don't cast a horrible spell on
my baby.'

'Would I ever do a thing like that?' said the fairy in a soft voice that reminded Queen Mo of a panther's purr. 'I have come to give Princess Rosie a rare and wonderful gift – the gift of beauty. When the Princess reaches her sixteenth birthday, she will look in a mirror and become the most beautiful princess in the world.'

The fairy waved her wand over the Princess's cradle, scattering black soot on the white blanket. And then she was gone.

'I don't know what to think,' said Queen Mo. 'It doesn't seem such a bad gift.'

The King wasn't so sure. 'Nothing good will come of Princess Rosie being beautiful,' he said. 'She will look down on everyone who is not as pretty as her.' And he passed a law that all mirrors should be banished from the kingdom forever to stop the fairy's spell from coming true.

Princess Rosie grew into a gentle and loving girl. She had two red pigtails that stuck out on either side of her head and her chubby face with its rosy cheeks was covered with freckles in summer. She was not beautiful, but she cheered everyone up with her smiling face and her marvellous jokes.

Sometimes she would catch a glimpse of herself smiling up from a pool of water or a stream, but she grew up not really knowing what she looked like.

For her sixteenth birthday treat, King Max and Queen Mo took Princess Rosie to a fair which was visiting the kingdom. Of course she was quite old enough to walk around the fair on her own and while King Max and Queen Mo were tucking into a cream tea, the Princess went off to look at the sideshows. There were coconut shies, roll-a-penny and hoop-la. The Princess bought some candy floss and felt very grown up, smiling and saying 'hello' to people without her mother and father by her side.

Suddenly she saw before her a large tent with a sign brightly painted in green and gold: HALL OF MIR-RORS. She looked around her. The crowds had not reached this corner of the fair yet. Princess Rosie was alone. There were pictures outside the tent of what you would look like in the mirrors – fat, thin, wiggly and straight. Underneath it said: YOU'VE NEVER SEEN YOURSELF LIKE THIS BEFORE – COME IN AND LAUGH YOURSELF SILLY.

Princess Rosie was curious to know what a mirror was, so she decided to take a look.

'How much is it to get in?' she asked the little old lady in grey who sat by the entrance.

'For you it's free, Your Highness,' said the little old lady, who tottered to her feet and nearly fell over on the grass as she made a low curtsey.

The Princess went inside. The tent was quite dark, lit by candles. She looked in the first mirror and giggled. Her head was huge and her body was skinny – like a lollipop. She looked in the next mirror. Her face was like a banana and her body like a squashed pumpkin. She began to roar with laughter and ran from one mirror to the next. Then she came to a mirror in a thick golden frame. She saw a lovely slim girl with long hair the colour of dawn and skin like milk. Princess Rosie's laughter stopped.

'I'm beautiful,' she whispered. 'I wish I could always look like this.'

All at once she heard a horrible shriek of laughter. The Hall of Mirrors disappeared. Princess Rosie found herself in the sunshine again, among the sideshows.

'Oh no,' cried Queen Mo, who realized at once what had happened when she saw the Princess.

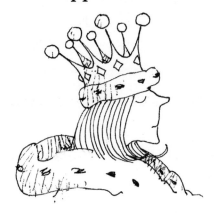

'What do you mean?' said Princess Rosie. 'Don't you think I'm beautiful? I'm a real princess at last. I don't want people to see me in rags like this. I should be dressed in silk and covered in diamonds.'

'What has happened to our darling Rosie, who was so sweet and kind?' sobbed the Queen.

'Don't call me Rosie,' snapped the Princess. 'From now on I expect to be called 'Your Royal Highness, the Princess Rosamunda.'

Back at the palace the Princess took a look around her. 'I'm going to make a few changes round here,' she said. 'This palace is a mess.'

'Your mother and I think it's wonderful,' stammered King Max.

'Wonderful?' shrieked Princess Rosamunda. 'I want a shiny glass palace with twenty-six floors and plastic plants. Let's knock this old one down.'

'But we can't afford to pay the builders,' said King Max.

'They'll have to work for nothing,' snapped Princess Rosamunda. 'Meanwhile I'm going shopping. I need new clothes and jewels. I need an expensive crown, too – one that will look good in all the pictures.'

King Max sat down on his throne. For the first time in years he looked sad. Queen Mo rushed to his side with a plate of cream cakes.

'Throw those horrible cakes out,' Princess Rosamunda ordered. 'No more cream cakes for you two from now on. I can't have parents that look like potato sacks. Whatever will the photographers say?'

Princess Rosamunda marched out of the room. She ordered the Prime Minister to banish all sweets and cream cakes from the land. She sent for the most expensive tailors in the country.

Because of her wild spending, King Max had to raise the taxes. The people became quite poor.

Soon many rich princes in shiny new sports cars came to ask for Rosamunda's hand in marriage. The Princess sent them packing. But she kept their presents.

One morning while the Princess was doing aerobics in the throne room, a young man wandered into the palace. Princess Rosamunda glared at him. He was fat, like her mother and father. His face was as red as a ripe tomato and his hair looked like a dog's dinner.

'Who let you into my palace?' demanded Princess Rosamunda.

'The door was open,' said the young lad. 'My name is Prince Cherubino and I'd like to marry you.'

'A prince?' sniffed the Princess. 'Princes wear smart clothes, not rags.'

'I'm different,' said Prince Cherubino happily. 'I only wear second-hand clothes.'

Princess Rosamunda was aghast. 'I suppose you've brought me a second-hand gift, too!' she said.

'The gift I have brought can't be seen or touched,' said Cherubino.

'What good is that?' asked the Princess.

'You're too rude to be a Princess,' replied Cherubino.

'You're too fat to be a Prince,' said Rosamunda. 'I wouldn't want to marry someone who looks like you.'

'I wouldn't marry you either,' said Cherubino. 'You're nothing but a bag of bones. I'd get bruises every time I gave you a hug!'

The Princess nearly laughed but stopped herself just in time.

'And if I kissed your frosty cheek, I'd get chilblains on my lips,' Cherubino added.

At this, the Princess could stop herself no longer and burst out laughing.

'This is the gift I bring, Princess,' said Cherubino, 'to be able to laugh at yourself.' And he sat on the steps of the throne and began to tell the Princess jokes. Princess Rosamunda tried hard not to laugh – it would smudge her lipstick. But Prince Cherubino hopped about like a frog. He told her jokes about hedgehogs and turtles. Princess Rosamunda roared with laughter.

King Max and Queen Mo rushed into the room. Cherubino offered them some cream cakes from his lunch box.

Princess Rosamunda was laughing so hard she didn't mind her parents eating cream cakes. She had one herself, too. Then she drank a bottle of lemonade.

Princess Rosamunda did agree to marry Cherubino, of course. Soon the wedding day arrived. Princess Rosamunda had to squeeze into one of Queen Mo's dresses to go to church because her own didn't fit her anymore. After the wedding everyone in the country was invited to a feast of chocolate fingers and banana ice-cream.

Then Prince Cherubino and Princess Rosamunda went to live in a baker's shop. Princess Rosamunda learnt how to make magnificent cream cakes while Prince Cherubino entertained the customers with his jokes. Life was much more comfortable there than in the horrible glass palace.

And although the fair came back each year, the Hall of Mirrors never returned to the kingdom again.